这本书属于

···

图书在版编目(CIP)数据

幼儿英文绘本 / (英) 梅兰妮·乔伊斯等著；(意) 玛瑞兹雅·鲁比诺等绘；郑晶译. -- 武汉：长江少年儿童出版社，2018.11
ISBN 978-7-5560-7373-3

Ⅰ.①幼… Ⅱ.①梅… ②玛… ③郑… Ⅲ.①儿童故事—图画故事—英国—现代 Ⅳ.①I561.85

中国版本图书馆CIP数据核字(2018)第015036号
著作权合同登记号：图字17-2018-060

大坏兔子

[英] 梅兰妮·乔伊斯 / 著　　[意大利] 玛瑞兹雅·鲁比诺 / 绘　郑　晶 / 译

责任编辑 / 佟　一　蒋　玲　赵　岚
装帧设计 / 肖　茜　美术编辑 / 魏嘉奇
出版发行 / 长江少年儿童出版社
经销 / 全国新华书店
印刷 / 佛山市顺德区帝图印刷有限公司
开本 / 787×1092　1 / 12　24印张
版次 / 2018 年 11 月第 1 版第 1 次印刷
书号 / ISBN 978-7-5560-7373-3
定价 / 180.00 元（全 12 册）

Big Bad Bunny

Written by Melanie Joyce, Illustrated by Maurizia Rubino
Published in 2014 by Igloo Books Ltd
Copyright © 2014 Igloo Books Ltd

本作品简体中文专有出版权经由 Chapter Three Culture 独家授权海豚传媒股份有限公司，由长江少年儿童出版社独家出版发行。版权所有，侵权必究。

策划 / 海豚传媒股份有限公司

邮箱 / dolphinmedia@vip.163.com　　网址 / www.dolphinmedia.cn
阅读咨询热线　027-87391723　　销售热线　027-87396822
海豚传媒常年法律顾问 / 湖北珞珈律师事务所　王清　027-68754966-227

CHAPTER3

Big Bad Bunny

大坏兔子

Reading Time 幼儿英文绘本

［英］梅兰妮·乔伊斯 / 著

［意大利］玛瑞兹雅·鲁比诺 / 绘

郑 晶 / 译

长江出版传媒 ｜ 长江少年儿童出版社

Beyond the wild-flower meadow,
in Cherry Blossom Wood,
the animals lived quietly
in their leafy neighbourhood.

在野花盛开的草地深处，有一片茂盛的樱花树林，
动物们在这里过着宁静的生活。

Life was simply perfect and
things were always the same.
Until one day a **stranger** arrived...

这里的生活简单、美好，事情按部就班。

直到有一天，来了一个陌生人……

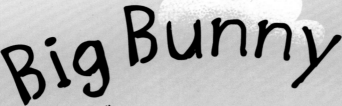

Big Bunny was his name.

…他的名字叫"大兔子"。

Big Bunny came bouncing by.

"I'm moving in here," he said.

大兔子蹦蹦跳跳地出现,"我要搬到这儿来。"他说。

He dug an enormous burrow
他挖了一个巨大的洞，

and flicked soil overhead.
泥土在他身后满天飞。

"What are **you** all staring at?"
boomed Big Bunny, looking around.
大兔子看了看四周，大声问道："你们都盯着我看什么？"

He thumped his back foot crossly
and dived down, underground.
他猛地一蹬后腿，钻进了地底下。

"Maybe he's just **shy**," said Owl. "It's not easy when you're new. Make Big Bunny welcome and he'll soon make friends with you."

"也许他有些害羞。"猫头鹰说，"搬到一个新的地方生活，不是那么容易的。如果能热情欢迎大兔子的到来，他很快就能和你们做朋友的。"

So, the field mice invited him to come for tea at four.

于是，田鼠们邀请他四点钟来喝茶。

They heard him *bounding* down the path...

他们听到大兔子沿着小路蹦蹦跳跳地跑来······

... and **thump** on their front door.

然后重重地敲着他们的前门。

Big Bunny had terrible manners.
He gobbled up all the food.

大兔子的用餐习惯很不好，他狼吞虎咽地把食物全吃光了。

He **chomped** on the cake
and **slurped** the cream.
He was really very rude.

他吧唧吧唧地吃着蛋糕，

然后又吸溜了一口奶油。

他实在是太粗鲁了。

"Come swimming with us," said the otters. "You'll think it's really cool."

"来和我们一起游泳吧。"水獭们说，"你一定会觉得非常棒。"

"Alright," said Big Bunny, giggling, but then...

"好的。"大兔子咯咯笑着，回应道。可就在这时……

... he **farted** in the pool.

他在水塘里放了一个屁。

When the baby badgers were napping, Big Bunny shouted...
当獾宝宝睡觉时，大兔子大喊一声："嘭！"

"BOO!"

"You naughty bunny," they squealed. "We've **had enough** of you!"
"你这只淘气的兔子！"大家尖叫起来，"我们受够你了！"

The animals of Cherry Blossom Wood
were cross and a little bit sad.
"We've tried our best," they said to Owl,
"but that Big Bunny is just so BAD!"

樱花树林里的动物们既生气又有点难过。

"我们已经尽力了。"大家对猫头鹰说，"可那只大兔子实在是太坏了！"

Owl sat and thought for a while.
"I've got a plan," he said. "We won't be mean to Bunny.
We'll do something **nice** instead."

猫头鹰坐着想了一会儿。"我有个主意。"他说，

"我们不要刻薄地对待大兔子，相反我们要做点友善的事情。"

Owl whispered to the animals
and everyone seemed delighted.
猫头鹰对动物们小声地说了一番话，大家看起来都很高兴。

They began to run all over the wood
and were terribly **excited**.
他们非常激动，开始满树林地奔忙起来。

The squirrels gathered nuts and the mice found lovely treats.

松鼠们搜集了许多坚果，老鼠们找到了美妙的食物。

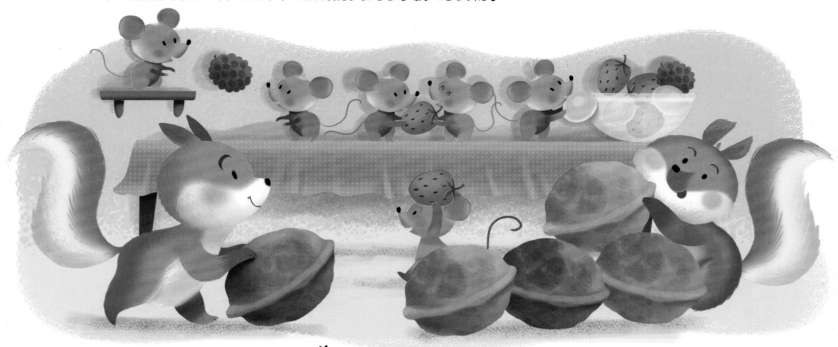

The badgers blew up balloons and the otters made some sweets.

獾们吹了很多气球，水獭们做了一些甜点。

In their den the little foxes all began to bake.

小狐狸们开始在洞穴里烤蛋糕。

"There's no time to lose," they said.
"There are lots of things to make."

"没时间浪费了。"他们说，"还有很多事情要做呢。"

The smells in Cherry Blossom Wood
were sugary and delicious. Big Bunny
got a **whiff** and soon became suspicious.

樱花树林里飘荡着香甜可口的气味。

大兔子吸了一口气，很快就开始怀疑起来。

"Something's up," he thought. "I definitely smell a rat. They're having fun **without me.** I'll put an end to that."

"一定是发生了什么事情。"他说，"我觉得非常可疑。他们背着我，自己玩得很开心，我要破坏这一切。"

He bounded into the clearing...
大兔子蹦跳着来到空地上，

... and hopped with one great **LEAP.**
纵身一跃。

"**Ah-ha!**" he cried,
"啊哈！"他大叫着，

bouncing off the jelly and landing in a heap.
从果冻上蹦下来，落在地上。

Big Bunny felt a bit silly, as everyone stood and stared.
"This is all for **YOU**," said Owl.
"We wanted to show you we cared."

当大家都站在那里盯着他的时候，大兔子觉得自己有点傻。

"这全都是为你准备的。"猫头鹰说，"我们想让你知道，我们很在乎你。"

"I'm sorry," said Big Bunny. He suddenly felt so sad.
"Cheer up!" cried the other animals. "You're really not **that** bad."

"对不起。"大兔子突然感到很难过。"高兴点！"其他的动物们喊道，"其实，你并没有那么坏！"

"Let's get the party started!" cried Owl.
"We'll make Big Bunny **welcome** here."
"Yes, please!" cried Big Bunny, bouncing, as everyone gave a cheer.

"立刻开始我们的派对吧！" 猫头鹰大声说道，"让我们热烈欢迎大兔子的到来。"

"真是太好了！" 大兔子一边跳，一边喊道。大家都欢呼起来。

Big Bunny was never bad after that, because he had **lots** of friends.

从那以后，大兔子再也没有使坏了，因为他交到了许多朋友。

Cherry Blossom Wood was **perfect** again and that is how the story ends!

樱花树林恢复了平和与美好。